NINJA SPY CATS

R.F. Kristi

Legal Notice

Published by: R.F. Kristi (www.IncaBooks.com) - First Edition

ISBN-13: 978-1546720294
ISBN-10: 1546720294

Edited by JK Mason

Illustrations by the group Videos Explainer

Book layout by ABC Media Solutions

Contents

1 - Curious News!

There was a flurry at our back door. The cat flap on the door suddenly popped open and Polo waddled in—all animated.

This was nothing new as Polo, our neighbor and friend, is excitable by nature. He just can't help himself. He is a pint-sized Pekingese pup who lives next door. He has been good friends with our family since we came over to London from Paris.

We were lazing about on our porch enjoying the first rays of sunshine. By "we," I mean myself, the pretty "purrrfect" Siberian kitty cat (if I may say so myself), the head of Missy's family; my sister Cara, a pretty Siamese kitty with bright blue eyes; and my diminutive but energetic brother Fromage, the cheese expert in the family. As usual, our adopted hamster Charlotte, Fromage's great buddy, was cuddled in his scarf snoozing away on Fromage's neck.

"Fromage!" Polo declared, shaking with excitement and waking us from our drowsy catnap on the sunny porch. "There is a rumor going around the park that you were seen doing a brilliant trapeze act among the branches of the trees."

Polo panted for a moment before continuing...

"A sight to behold. You pirouetted amongst the branches like a professional trapeze actor, performing each move with ease and precision, like a real expert circus performer."

Illustration 1: In comes Polo our excitable Pekingese neighbor.

Polo paused for dramatic effect...

"At the end of the show, you took off your beret and made a deep bow to the doggies watching below before strutting off with your tail high in the air, and then you disappearing into the treetops."

A few more pants from Polo...

"Quite a cocky performance, I understand. I am just coming from the park where you are the talk of the town with the doggy kingdom residents as they take their walks in the park. It was as if you were thumbing your nose at the doggies with a Catch-Me-If-You-Dare challenge!"

"I met Terrance while out for a run, and he confirmed the rumor. He had seen your performance. I missed it as I took my stroll later than usual. Is there any chance I could see an encore?"

Polo said this with his tiny pink tongue hanging out, his round bright eyes filled with expectation. He was referring to Kensington Park, of course, which was just next door to us, where the neighborhood doggies went for their daily walks or runs with their owners. Kensington Park was a haven for doggy chitchat. The doggies not only took their walks in the park but also had the opportunity to exchange stories and generally gossip to their hearts content with the other doggies out in the park.

You wouldn't imagine the stories we have heard through Polo about the neighborhood goings-on. Polo is a talkative bundle of energy, and he hangs around more with the gossipy circle of doggies.

"That's impossible," I scoffed before Fromage had a chance to open his sleepy eyes. "Fromage has not moved from the house today. He didn't even visit the cheese shop as Missy was on a short business trip for the day."

Cara sat up and started washing her already immaculate petite face and said with a grin, "Fromage performing a trapeze act!!! Now that is something I would like to see."

Illustration 2: Cara looks on disapprovingly at Fromage's clumsy handiwork.

It was true. Fromage, our lovable brat of a brother, is anything but agile. He can't even walk on the ledge of a bath tub without accidentally falling in the water. He is prone to mishaps. We love him dearly but he is a clumsy little fur ball.

Fromage prides himself more on being a cheese connoisseur. His main interest in life is cheese and anything related to cheese. He never tires when talking about his cheese projects. This is mainly in reference to the cheese shops our family owns in Paris and London. Fromage is the mascot of our London cheese shop and restaurant, and he is extremely proud of this fact.

Polo looked uncertainly at Fromage, who was lying sleepily in the sun. Even goodhearted Polo couldn't deny that Fromage was clumsy.

Just then Monk slipped in through the cat flap and opened the door for Terrance to enter. Monk and Terrance are part of Inca & Company, the detective agency I lead. They live in the main house, the grand mansion. Our cottage is at the bottom of the gardens of this mansion.

Monk is a portly but elegant Russian Blue cat. Despite his size, he does manage to enter through our cat flap. But he needs to open the door for Terrance and is clever at doing so. Terrance would never fit through our cat door.

Terrance is the original detective on our team. He is a large, swanky golden retriever. His owner, Solo is a real live detective too. In fact, a world-famous detective, and Terrance helps him solve crimes along with Hobbs, Solo's manservant.

Illustration 3: Terrance and Monk, friends for life.

Terrance is a courageous partner to Solo and has appeared in the newspapers for his bravery in helping Solo solve crimes. Solo, with help from Terrance, is well known for helping the police crack important cases. Hobbs, Terrance's keeper and right-hand to

Solo, usually plays a low-key role in the world-famous detective agency.

In fact, I had decided to form my own furry detective agency after getting tangled in a case involving the recovery of a valuable diamond necklace. I had become very interested in solving crimes. Solo was my role model.

At the moment, sleuthing was in my blood.

"What's this news about Fromage?" asked Monk. Apparently, Terrance had passed on the news to him, as well.

Terrance barked, "Fromage, what a show you performed for the doggies at Kensington park this morning! Want to give us a repeat performance?"

Fromage sat up sleepily. "I can give you my wonderful Ninja cat performance for sure," he replied, all the sleepiness disappearing rapidly.

Fromage, in addition to his love of cheese, has had a bee in his bonnet about becoming a Ninja cat since he saw the movie *Ninja Turtles* on television.

Saying so, Fromage carefully set Charlotte down by me and quickly took up his famous Ninja position with a loud meow, looking more like a hissing tea pot in my opinion than a Ninja warrior.

I couldn't help but hide my smile behind my paws. Since our return from Provence, France, where we were involved with art thieves, whenever he gets an opportunity, he loves to show off as Fromage the Ninja cat.

He took his Ninja cat stance again, ready to roll about the room meowing "Hee Yaah"as he throws his arms and legs about.

"Hee Yaah" is his standard mantra or chant when he becomes a Ninja cat.

Without much ado, he did his usual performance, knocking down the cushions that were tastefully arranged on our sitting room sofas by Missy. He then nearly overturned the large flower arrangement on the side table. His actions caused both Cara and I to leap on the table to steady and preserve the beautiful arrangement adorning the table.

Silence fell over the audience!

Even Terrance, who had witnessed the performance at the Kensington gardens, could not believe it was Fromage who was responsible for the polished performance he had witnessed a short while ago. Terrance rubbed is eyes in confusion, shook his great head, and looked at me helplessly.

"I could have sworn it was Fromage," was all he could mutter. "He even cheekily doffed his beret at us doggies and bowed deeply from his waist, before trotting off with his tail held high," he continued.

Polo excitedly yapped, "I got it! I got it! It was Fromage's super-natural spirit floating out of himself and performing acrobatic stunts in the Kensington park."

We all looked at Fromage who had collapsed like a half-melted Popsicle after his performance as a Ninja cat. He had a satisfied, if not somewhat smug expression on his face.

Illustration 4: A hissing tea pot in action - that's our Fromage!

I will give him that much: Fromage is cocky and sure of himself and proud of his abilities. To our mind, he looked nothing like what he imagined he represented while performing his Ninja cat moves. I could well imagine from his dreamy expression that he could hear the deafening applause of his adoring fans. But he heard nothing of the skepticism in our voices!

I shook my head. "I don't think so Polo." I said. "If Fromage's super-natural spirit was floating around, he would be going after cheese instead of those antics in Kensington Park. There has to be another explanation."

I thought to myself, "How could Fromage be in two places at the same time? Above all, how could he be so agile?"

It was a mystery indeed! My beautifully balanced whiskers twitched in anticipation. I was keen to get to the bottom of this puzzle. I am curious by nature and need to know everything happening. I definitely had to find out who this Fromage look-alike was!

I looked at Fromage thoughtfully, going over the possibilities in my mind. I decided to wait and watch, and do some snooping around before openly revealing my thoughts. With this in mind, I sidled up to Polo and asked him to spread the word around among his doggy pals to keep an eye out for this acrobatic Fromage lookalike kitty cat.

After watching Solo, I had learned that a good sleuth does not just throw around theories. One has to make inquiries first.

Illustration 5: In the mind of Fromage, a suave and polished Ninja cat is he!

2 - Is Something Happening at the French Embassy?

That evening Missy returned home rather late. We awaited her arrival impatiently. Home was never really home without Missy in it. She is a loving and caring, bouncing bundle of joy—our very own humanoid! Cara, Fromage and I jointly own her although she tends to think that she owns us. Misguided humanoid that she is!

Missy is energetic and charismatic, in our opinion, and she cares for us a great deal. Our family would not be complete without her.

As usual, while she prepared dinner, we hung around the kitchen as she recounted the day's happenings, Fromage more often than not getting tangled under her feet. But Missy truly loves him. He rarely gets a scolding, even if he breaks something, which in fact is quite often.

Illustration 6: The family in our cozy kitchen!

Missy sees past his innate clumsiness. All she sees is a round, adorable ball of fur who loves cheese. All types of cheese! Fromage is our mascot and so far, the cheese business was doing very well indeed!

Missy has a soft spot for our furry family. She thinks we are perfect. She is not wrong there; we are perfect of course, with the exception of Fromage, who tends to be rather clumsy. He makes up for his clumsiness one-hundredfold, according to Missy, with his cheese connoisseur skills.

Recently, there was another successful milestone in the history of our cheese store and restaurant in London! Missy had been successful a few months ago in obtaining a new contract with the French Embassy to cater their wine and cheese parties. Since the embassy had frequent parties, catering to the diplomatic circle had proved to be a winner.

Missy had discussed with her French partners, Genevieve and Jacques, and they had jointly agreed that she would concentrate on growing this side of the business. They knew that if catering to the French Embassy was a success, they would garner more business with other embassies.

Representatives from several embassies had approached her already, and the cheese sales and restaurant had expanded to include catering services. The catering service was moving along well under Missy's management.

Naturally, Fromage took credit for this success and said that "he," being the mascot of the London cheese venture, had made all the difference in the world to our business and to Missy's expansion of the operation. Cara just rolled her eyes when Fromage started bragging about this.

But we all knew in our hearts that Fromage was passionate about the cheese trade, and his presence at the shop and restaurant drew a lot of customers to the vicinity.

Missy explained the arrangements she had made for an important party to be held at the French Embassy. Fromage nodded his head in approval when she mentioned the types of cheese she would be serving at this event. She said all the waiters—with herself included—must undergo a thorough security check because important dignitaries were to attend this party.

She tilted her head to one side and said, "I bumped into Solo this morning coming out of the French Embassy. I wonder what he was doing there? I was going to ask, but his face was serious, so I didn't want to be nosey."

Not nosey? I have no problems being nosey. I am inquisitive by nature and a thoughtful expression came over my face.

"Solo visiting the French Embassy!!! Could it be that they had called him in professional-ly?"

I whispered to the gang, "Let's go over at midnight to our headquarters. I want to check with Terrance to see if he knows what's going on. Fromage, can you slip over to Monk's after dinner and tell Terrance and him that we should have a meeting tonight?"

We used Monk and Terrance's grand library with a cozy fireplace as our headquarters. The library is rarely used after midnight, and during cold winters was warm and comfy after a full day of logs merrily roasting in the fire place.

Fromage nodded his head and disappeared out the window. He didn't wish to wait until dinnertime. He soon returned nodding and signaling that the meeting was on. Monk had promised to pass the message to Polo so that he could join us.

3 - Pow-Wow at Midnight!

Missy worked hard all day long! By habit, we went to bed early and woke up early too, around 5:30 in the morning. Before long Missy was fast asleep allowing us to softly leave the room through our cat flap and race to Monk's house.

The large mansion was silent. We quietly padded to the library and the other members of Inca & Company were in their usual places and quietly whispering. They greeted us with a warm welcome! There was no doubt about it. Monk, Terrance and Polo were happy to be part of my detective team.

I had two issues to discuss: First, try to find out from Terrance why Solo visited the French Embassy. Second, determine if Polo and Terrance's doggy friends who visited the park had seen Fromage's lookalike in the park once again. The second question about Fromage's double was settled quickly as no one had seen him again.

But Terrance had more information as to why Solo had visited the Embassy. He said: "Do you know anything about spies?"

Illustration 7: A shadowy spy!

We remained silent.

Taking our silence as a negative response, Terrance continued: "A spy collects information about an enemy's plans. He or she tries to learn as much as possible about the enemy and then pass the information to his or her own side."

Terrance continued, with his face in a thoughtful frown: "Important documents have gone missing from the embassy. Information has been obtained that these documents will be given to an outside source that could cause serious damage to the security of the free world. The suspicion is that there will be an attempt to pass the documents during a diplomatic gathering soon."

Terrance growled: "Solo said that if the documents fall into the wrong hands, it would be disastrous for the free world."

I snapped back, "Solo suspects that the documents will be passed at the party Missy is catering at the embassy this coming weekend, isn't that it?"

Fromage quickly explained about Missy's new business venture, providing the catering services to the diplomatic circles around town.

I was itching to get us into this affair and assist Solo. Could we do it? I wondered, deep in thought. I guess Monk saw the uncertainty in my eyes.

"Remember how we retrieved the stolen painting in Paris, Inca?" he meowed to me. "You can do anything you set your mind out to do."

"Very generous of you Monk. But remember we had Amador's assistance."

The team looked at me expectantly. They had respect for me as their chief and they always allowed me to make the final decision on if we would accept a case or not. So far, we had succeeded in all the cases we were involved in. But this was a Biggy! International espionage was really something in a different league.

I am a smart kitty and after all, Solo was on the case. He had become my hero after he helped recover a valuable painting stolen while under the care of Aunt Florence. We had a lot to do with that recovery, but unbeknownst to Solo, we had proved to be a valuable asset to him in solving this case.

I never missed an opportunity to observe Solo from a distance. I knew he was puzzled as to why he had two watchful eyes on him at all times. I sometimes see him uneasily looking around. Once he even caught me hiding behind the curtains.

I know that Solo admires me. Who can blame him? I am a very pretty kitty with intelligent round eyes and a beautiful bushy tail that falls like a luxurious feather. All he did was pick me up and ask, "What are you doing here Inca? Searching for your friend Monk?"

I am aware that Monk suspects me of watching Solo. But he says nothing. Monk adores Solo. I guess he thought it only natural that I would also.

I decided!

"You are right Terrance," I said. "We cannot abandon a case offered to us on a silver platter. No matter the level of challenge we may face!"

The whole gang had something to say.

From Polo, an excitable yap: "Wonderful! This is something to tell my doggy friends at the park. They love to hear about our adventurous escapades."

From Cara: "Here goes our peace again...Good decision, Inca. After all, we don't want Missy's new venture to be spoiled because of this drama."

She was right! Missy was involved as well as she would be on the premises. Fromage had a dreamy expression on his face. I knew he was picturing himself in his Ninja costume attacking and conquering the enemy single handedly.

Only Charlotte remained silent. But she knew that she could be very useful to us due to her small size and ability to get into places that none of us could fit into. There was no doubt about it. Charlotte was a valuable member of the Inca & Company Detective Agency—ever ready to follow my lead. I knew I could count on her one hundred percent.

Terrance said, It's a done deal. We will be assisting Solo, unknown to him. Let's go to the French Embassy so we can case it out tomorrow night....I will get more information by that time. Solo and Hobbs will surely be discussing the information they have and their next move."

4 - The Plot Thickens!

As usual, we woke up very early the next morning. All was calm in the Missy household! Missy and Cara did their yoga stances first thing in the morning. Sometimes Fromage tried his hand at some yoga moves too but was hopeless at it; even so, that never prevents him from trying, and Missy is a bundle of encouragement, urging him on.

However, today Fromage was in a dreamy mood whispering to Charlotte about how he could become the most famous Ninja cat in the universe. The only Ninja cat who was a cheese expert! He had a ready audience in Charlotte who listened to her friend, her whiskers twitching as a sign of support.

I went to see if there were croquettes still available in our bowl, the large red bowl we jointly share. I took a quick bite in anticipation of my salsa practice as soon as the yoga session was over.

After the yoga session, while Missy was preparing her breakfast, the cozy cottage was rife with the beat of salsa music, and I started my dance practice.

'Olé! Olé!' I mewed, practicing my dance moves, while the rest of the gang watched me in silent admiration, and Missy observed me in delight. They never seemed to tire of my dancing.

I had a new member in my audience: Monk knew our morning program, and made it a point to watch me dance every morning. I had offered to teach him the salsa, but he seemed to prefer *watching* me dance. I guess I am a pretty sight as I am a nifty salsa dancer.

Illustration 8: A morning yoga session with Cara and Missy

You may have noted that modesty is not one of my virtues.

Later that morning, while we were lying on our sunny porch, Terrance joined us.

"Solo had found out that a master spy was coming from Prague. It would be the responsibility of the master spy to retrieve the documents from where they wre placed in hiding and take them off the premises. Solo said that he must prevent this at all costs and retrieve the documents himself."

"Where is Prague?" asked Fromage.

Charlotte responded, "Prague is the capital city of the Czech Republic, just like Paris is the capital city of France and London is the capital city of the United Kingdom."

Polo added, "It is close to France and in Eastern Europe. I have visited with the Señora."

Polo had been all around the world with the Señora and her wealthy husband. He himself was rescued by Raoul, the Señora's husband, and handed over as a gift to the beautiful Señora. The Señora was a former famous opera singer.

Terrance continued, "Solo has to be very careful though as everything must be done hush hush to avoid a diplomatic incident."

The Master Spy, I thought to myself. This had an interesting ring to it. I wondered what the Master Spy looked like and how he planned to get into the French Embassy and retrieve the documents. I imagined a sinister figure slithering from pillar to post with the intent of stealing secret documents. A mysterious figure always moving in the shadows.

My heart started beating faster. I smelled danger! "Delicious!" I was itching to get into the middle of this case. I was anxious to get on the premises myself and check out the French Embassy. Although we now lived in London, we still considered ourselves French cats. After all, we carried French passports.

Illustration 9: The salsa expert, that's me?

We were on our forth detective case now and I was quivering with excitement. I was careful not to show my joy at the thought of being embroiled in another case. I believed in keeping a cool demeanor just like Solo.

We had agreed to meet outside our cottage at midnight. In the meantime, Missy left for the restaurant with Fromage riding in the basket of her bicycle. Cara, Charlotte and I went out to our sunny porch to enjoy the sun. Monk joined us soon after as Terrance was out and about with Hobbs. Terrance was a working dog, a top detective dog, and his mornings were taken up with Hobbs and Solo.

I stretched out on the sunny porch dreamily thinking of our escapade tonight. We had agreed that Terrance would take us to the premises since he knew the location of the embassy. When we arrived there, I would take over and lead the kitties in the group and Charlotte over the wall and into the compound.

Terrance had already given me a layout of the building and I was hoping that we kitties would be able to scale the wall without too much trouble. There were a few sturdy trees against the walls, as described by Terrance.

There was a buzz at our back door and a small round face with a little pink tongue poked his head through our cat door. It was Polo! "Can I bring a friend in to meet you all?" he asked.

Illustration 10: A visit from Polo's friend Gordin.

I walked over to the back door and poked my head out of the cat door to see who it was.

"Inca meet Gordin," said Polo.

"Gordin, here is Inca, the head of our detective team," he said proudly, as if he was introducing a queen to a commoner. Polo does wonders to my ego!

I had heard about Gordin from Polo before. Gordin was a friend of Polo's from his rescue home days. Gordin was a small dog, just like Polo. Perhaps slightly bigger than Polo and I. He lived in the vicinity and met Polo at Kensington Park where they went for walks every morning.

Gordin had a colorful history. He was born in Spain and then moved to Germany with his owners. For some sad reason, he ended up in a rescue home in Germany until—for his good fortune—he was spotted by a kind Englishman and brought over to London. Polo told us that Gordin's doggy passport claims he is a Brittany Spaniel, but Polo suspects he is of mixed parentage.

I looked at Gordin carefully. He was small but sturdy with a white body and brown patches artistically arranged on his face and body. Just like his friend Polo, he was a friendly and trusting looking doggy. Sometimes I am amazed at these doggies, who are so willing to be friends with anyone and everyone without hesitation, unlike us kitties.

Gordin greeted me with his tail waving rapidly, thumping the floor like a wild drum beat. He nearly licked me in his enthusiasm at meeting me, but he pulled himself back just in time, when Polo gave him a warning look.

Polo got it right, alright. Being friends with a doggy is one thing, but I certainly drew the line at having myself licked.

"Hello, Gordin!" I said, keeping my distance in case he got carried away in his enthusiasm and tried to lick me again.

"Hola, mi bellaza!" said Gordin.

Polo translated: "Gordin said 'Hello beautiful,' in Spanish."

Polo's Señora and Raoul are Spanish and they often speak to each other and to Polo in Spanish. Hence Polo and Gordin often speak in Spanish as Gordin was born in Spain and considers himself Spanish and never fails to speak the language when he gets a chance.

"Come on in and meet the rest of my family and Monk."

"Monk is an old friend," Gordin added with a soft raspy bark.

Monk waved to him casually and said, "How do you do, Gordin? I have not seen you for some time. Is everything OK?"

Polo jumped in by yapping: "Gordin has some news. That's why I invited him over. Go ahead, Gordin. Tell them what you told me."

Gordin sat down on the porch and looked at each of us through melting brown eyes. His black nose twitching!

"Polo had told me about Fromage, the cat who performed a superb trapeze act in the park a few days ago, and asked me to keep an eye out for him."

"It was not Fromage, Gordin," I quickly intervened. "But please continue with the story as we are all keen to hear about it."

"Well then, let's call him the X-Factor," added Monk.

"He may not be Fromage," Gordin continued. "But he looked exactly like the cat in the photo over there." He pointed at a photo of Fromage proudly sitting in front of a large platter of cheese and fruit. The one that Missy had taken on the day the restaurant-cum-shop first opened its doors. "He too sports a French beret."

Illustration 11: The X-Factor - an expert acrobat in action!

After a pause, Gordin continued: "In any case, last evening, I had gone for a walk with my master in the gardens and as usual while he was chatting with a friend, I went to snoop around the trees, when suddenly I felt a pair of beady eyes watching me from amongst the bushes. I must admit that a chill went down my spine."

He paused for a second then continued: "It was the daring cat we had observed a few days ago.... All he did though was a great somersault, as if to show off to me. He then tipped his beret at me, as he had last time and silently moved away with hardly a ripple or glance in my direction."

Gordin looked around at us, making sure we were listening. Then he continued: "I knew that Polo and his friends were very interested in the X-Factor, so I started following him, moving softly from one tree trunk to the next. I saw him enter a small white house across the street from the park and disappear from sight.... I made sure to mark the house so I could return to it again with you all," he said.

Polo caught my eye and grinned at me. "You know how we doggies mark our territory, don't you Inca," he yapped.

I saw Cara blush, and then Monk—noticing her embarrassment—quickly changed the subject. He said, "Good job Gordin; quick thinking! You have to show us the X-Factor's domicile! I know that Inca and all of us would very much like to meet him."

We had already made plans to visit the French Embassy that night, so with reluctance, I told my eager troupe that we would visit the home of the X-Factor the following day. After thanking Gordin for his services, we bid him goodbye and promised that we would see him again soon. He departed saying, "You are welcome, Inca. Any friend of Polo's is a friend of mine. I am glad to be of service to you."

Illustration 12: Fromage in his world of cheese!

5 - The Journey Begins

That night we met under the stars outside our cottage. It was a clear night. The month of May is pleasant in London. The weather was mild and the flowers were blooming in the neighboring parks and gardens. The air smelled fresh and sweet.

London has a habit of suddenly pouring with rain even during the mild month of May. But fortunately, today we had experienced an average of eight hours of sunshine, so the pavements were warm under our paws and appeared as if paved in gold due to the yellow light from the street lamps.

Terrance led the way as we padded after him. He had a habit of galloping rather fast. But we kitties were in good shape with our daily practice of yoga, salsa, and in Fromage's case his new love: practicing being a Ninja cat.

Only Monk was rotund by nature, but he was strong and had longer legs than the rest of us kitties. So, all in all, we moved along at a brisk pace.

Polo is blessed with short stumpy legs. Nevertheless, he kept up too. He was in good form as he was walked every day by his Señora. I was pleased to note that we were a sporty bunch of furry detectives.

It was not a long walk. It took us about 15 minutes to reach Knightsbridge from Kensington where the French Embassy was located. We had passed an enormous building which Polo pointed out was the Victoria and Albert Museum he had visited with the Señora. Polo was a culture buff having not only traveled the world but also visited many museums large and small with his beloved Señora.

"One day, when I was not on a mission, I would enter the Victoria and Albert Museum to check out what Polo was crooning about," I vowed to myself.

We arrived at a great white building with the French flag matching Fromage's scarf gently waving in the night breeze.

"What a majestic building!" said Monk.

Fromage saluted our flag saying, "Vive la France!" meaning long live France! or hurray for France!

Terrance had done his job, and done it well, bringing us to the embassy without once getting lost. He and Polo had retreated behind a wall on the opposite side of the building and settled down under a nearby bush. They would keep watch from under the bush.

The moon hung low in the sky. I eyed the building and considered the best way to enter. There were grills all around the building, and I realized it would be much better to slip through the grills rather than daring to climb over the sharp pointed iron bars.

So that's exactly what I did, waving at the others to follow me; and without much ado, we were inside the compound of the French Embassy. I made my way to the rear of the building, gesturing the others to follow silently behind me.

At the back, a set of stairs led down to a cellar with an open window. We silently sprang into the building through the open window and made our way upstairs. What a splendid interior furnished in the typical French style with beautiful French antique furniture!

Illustration 13: A majestic building – the French Embassy!

"Swell!" said Monk, and the team members who had crossed over from Paris to London, swelled with pride.

There was no one around, and we bounded up the large stairs admiring the premises. It was such a big building; how on earth would we find out where the documents were hidden? Suddenly I had an idea! I looked at Charlotte thoughtfully. *Would Fromage agree to part with Charlotte?* I wondered.

I said, "The best way to find out what is going on is for one of us to stay for a few days inside this building and observe what is happening." I looked at Charlotte "Are you game for it, Charlotte?"

Charlotte had a pleased look on her face. She seemed to relish the idea that it was she who had been chosen from the team for this extremely critical task. "Yes, indeed I would be game for it. I will be: 'Charlotte, the hamster spy, the smallest spy in the world,' she said. "If there is anything to discover here Inca, you can count on me!"

Fromage looked at me anxiously. "Inca, I can't leave her behind all alone. It may be too dangerous! I will stay behind as well to protect her."

"Protect me!" Charlotte drew herself up to her full height, which was not very high at all. "I can look after myself! Thank you very much Fromage!" she snapped, indignantly.

I explained to Fromage: "Charlotte can hide unnoticed and observe what is going on. If you or any one of us stays behind, we will surely be spotted." After a moment, I added: "We will visit to see that she is well!"

The others nodded in agreement, and I said, "The cocktail party is tomorrow night. If the documents are to be passed to the Master Spy, it will surely be done tomorrow night. Charlotte need not stay here alone too long."

There was no hesitation in accepting my decision, and so it was decided!

Illustration 14: A pow wow with Monk in the French Embassy.

6 - Face-to-Face with the X-Factor!

Ensuring that Charlotte was in a safe space in the French Embassy, out of the view of human eyes, we returned home promising to return the next night around midnight! We were a somber team walking back, all of us worried about Charlotte.

Terrance whispered to me, "Wise decision Chief! We have our very own spy inside the French Embassy. It's the best way to find out exactly what is happening in there. Smart move!"

"Thank you, Terrance" I whispered back. "But I hope Charlotte is safe! If anything happens to her, I will never forgive myself."

Monk heard my comment and came back behind me and nuzzled my worried face. "Charlotte is a brave lass, Inca. Only yesterday she was telling me about her escapades from the basement of the science lab in Paris. She can handle herself very well, and we will go over tomorrow night, as soon as it is dark."

Terrance had decided to lead us back through the park. Daylight was gently falling. It was very early in the morning. Still too early for anyone to be around.

We were back home before Missy woke up!

Illustration 15: Walking back through the park!

Today was the day the cocktail party would be held at the Embassy. She was in a mad rush to get to the restaurant where her team was gathering to prepare the trays of cheese and wine to be taken to the Embassy.

It was a hurried breakfast, and she absentmindedly filled our food trays and water dishes, including Charlotte's, without noticing that Charlotte was not in the kitchen.

I knew that Fromage was missing his companion, who usually cuddled in his shawl when he took a nap or moved out of the cottage. To take his mind off Charlotte, I had asked Polo to ask Gordin to take us to the building the X-Factor entered.

I was curious to find out who the X-Factor was. He wore a French beret, just like Fromage and I suspected that he was probably of French origin.

What was he doing in London?

Why did he resemble Fromage to the extent that even Terrance thought it was Fromage?

These were some of the questions revolving around my mind.

When Gordin walked in later with Polo, without much ado, we silently followed him in search of the white building he had marked where he last saw the X-Factor enter. Terrance was on duty today and hence not able to come with us. We had been used to following Terrance, who was a professional search-and-rescue dog. He had received diplomas and medals for his achievements in this sphere.

Watching Gordin at work was rather amusing and quickly took our minds off Charlotte. He sniffed the ground moving in all directions. After following him in circles and arriving back at the starting spot several times, with Polo throwing us apologetic glances, I decided to sit under a shady bush in the park with Fromage and Cara and asked Polo to come back for us as soon as Gordin found the trail he was searching for.

It was another warm sunny day and the park was a pleasant place to sit in and take a quick cat nap. We were tired after our previous night's escapade about town. Fromage, Cara and I curled up under a bush, the warm sun bathing and warming our bones. We kitties love the warmth.

It seemed to me that nearly an hour had gone by when Polo came panting up to us. "Come quick, Inca" he barked. "Gordin found the building. There is a delivery truck parked in front and the side door is open. There is no one about and you can go into the building through the open back door."

We scampered after his heels and with a hasty thanks to Gordin ran into the building before the delivery man came out and closed the door.

We had decided that Polo and Gordin would stay outside across the street in the park. They settled down under a droopy willow tree. We had discussed that it would be easier for us kitties to escape from the premises if the delivery man left and the back door was closed.

There were four of us inside the building: Monk, Cara, Fromage and I. We decided to split into twos at the entrance: Cara and I to examine the downstairs while Fromage and Monk took the upstairs.

Cara followed me and we hid under the staircase as the delivery man came out from the cellar and left through the open door, shutting it behind. There seemed to be nobody around. The house was silent.

We cautiously came out of hiding, looked around, and then entered through a door into the kitchen. We stopped in our tracks, our faces in astonishment! Fromage was calmly sitting, hunched over and having a snack from a food bowl of aromatic croquettes in the kitchen. We caught the scent of the savory snack from where we stood spellbound.

Cara exclaimed, "Fromage! Eating again! You were not supposed to leave Monk's side."

"Can you never stop thinking about food?" she added.

Fromage looked at us in surprise, but then he removed his beret and bowed deeply to us and said, "Welcome pretty kitties! What brings you here? You are welcome to share my food if that is why you are here."

We stopped in our tracks with looks of astonishment! He *looked* like Fromage, he *sounded* like Fromage, but we slowly realized that he was NOT Fromage.

This must be the X-Factor!!!

Here was Fromage's double, certainly! But a more polished version of our little brother.

The X-Factor had a neat waistline. He was also more elegant, unlike our sloppy and casually dressed brother. His beret and scarf—which were very similar to the ones Fromage wore, depicting the French flag—were in immaculate condition.

Hearing our voices, Monk and Fromage ran down the stairs and stopped in amazement! Fromage was the most surprised! The two lookalikes stared at each other in shocked silence!

"Camembert?" whispered one lookalike, and the other whispered "Beaufort, is that you?"

Our Fromage dashed up to the other Fromage and wrapped him in a great big hug, tears pouring down his whiskers. He turned to us and said "This is my brother Camembert! I would recognize him anywhere."

Camembert responded, "I heard about a cat that looked like me—and the doggies in the park kept calling me Fromage. I see you have changed your name from Beaufort to Fromage! It somehow suits you well, little brother."

Quick introductions were made all around.

I had suspected as such all along, as I recall Missy telling us that Fromage had a twin brother who had been adopted first when his parents moved with the first owners of our cheese shop in Paris. But how is it that two brothers could be so opposite in agility?!

Fromage was as agile as a wet mop, while here was his brother Camembert, who moved with such grace and precision. But there was no doubt about it: they were brothers. Twins to be precise, as similar as two peas in a pod. I sincerely hoped that for the sake of our sweet natured little brother that Camembert was good natured like Fromage.

The two brothers had a lot of catching up to do, and we left them to themselves, sitting together, happily watching them gossip and laugh, remembering their parents and telling each other what each of them had been doing since parting.

Suddenly, we remembered that Polo and Gordin were waiting for us across the street. Reluctantly, I had to stop the chatter and remind Fromage that we needed to get home before Missy returned. It was tonight that she was catering for the cocktail party at the French Embassy and she would surely come home before leaving once again to organize the party.

I also reminded Fromage that we needed to visit Charlotte, and this finally got him moving. With reluctance, the two brothers said their goodbyes. We parted ways, promising to catch up with Camembert again.

On the way back, Cara and I were curious to find out more about Camembert, but Fromage could not tell us very much. It appeared that Fromage had spent all the time talking about us, his family, and the cheese business.

All he had gathered was that Camembert was attached to a diplomat and had traveled to many countries since leaving his parents and Fromage in the Paris cheese shop. They had arrived a few weeks ago in London.

7 - Cocktails at the Embassy!

Back at home, we found Missy was dressed and ready for her work assignment. We couldn't help but admire her in the attire she would wear to manage the cocktail party at the French Embassy that evening. She was dressed in flat black ballerina shoes, a slim fitting pair of black pants, and a crisp white shirt with a string of her favorite pearls around her slender neck.

She did not stay long at home, but wished us a rushed goodbye after ensuring that our dinner was served. Soon after she left, Monk, Terrance and Polo arrived, and we left home and made our way through the park to the embassy.

As we walked, Terrance informed us that Solo was attending the cocktail party at the embassy and he had confirmed information that the document would be retrieved tonight.

When we arrived at the embassy, we made sure that Missy did not see us. There was quite a hustle and bustle both at the back door and the main entrance of the superb white building. We observed many cars driving up, and well-dressed persons entering the building for the party. Missy and her staff of six were busy moving from the kitchen to the banquet hall carrying trays with wine and platters of cheese.

There were about twenty guests in the beautiful hall, all formally dressed, with the gentlemen in black suits and the ladies in high heels and long elegant and expensive looking dresses. There was the sound of lightly clinking wine glasses and soft chatter around the room.

Terrance and Polo had trotted over with us, but did not enter the building. They were sitting under a bush, discretely watching the events from a distance. They knew they could not enter the premises without being noticed, whereas we kitties were small and could hide easily.

Solo was amongst the guests looking trendy in black. Missy, as she was on duty, did not stop to speak to him, though I observed his gaze following her with a twinkle in his eye.

Cara and I looked at each other with a knowing smile.

The kitties in my family were sure that Solo liked our Missy very much indeed. I wondered if Monk and Terrance had not guessed how much he liked her. We approved of course, although Cara did not very much relish the thought of sharing Missy with another humanoid. She felt she already had to share Missy with the two of us, and another human or animal would be too much.

Us kitties had entered through the back and were discretely hidden under the stairs. When the cocktail party was in full swing, Fromage went in search of Charlotte. He found her on the landing under a hole in the carpet, and he let out a sigh of relief when she slid into his scarf.

I believe he felt naked if she was not safely hidden in his scarf. Fromage is very protective of Charlotte. They had been friends even before Fromage joined our family. I guess you could say that Charlotte was his nearest and dearest friend.

But this time she didn't stay in his scarf long. She slid off and turned to me as soon as they arrived under the stairs. "What a night it was," she whispered.

We gathered around her to listen to what she had to say.

"It was a busy night indeed," said Charlotte, her little nose quivering with excitement. "Soon after all of you left, there was a sudden movement in the quiet premises, and I observed a strange person slithering into the building through the downstairs window, followed by another small slithery figure."

"The figure was dressed in black. From what I could see in the shadowy light, she resembled a tall, lean human cat. She was accompanied by a real Ninja cat, added Charlotte, giving Fromage an apologetic look."

"I didn't mean to insult you Fromage, but this Ninja cat looked as if he meant business. They both looked so menacing. I am normally not afraid, but the sight of these ghostly figures was a shock to my system. I was frozen with fear."

"But I was in a good position... hidden under the carpet on the landing of the staircase and I could see both the upstairs and downstairs. I stayed completely still, only letting my eyes move."

"I was happy to be small. Thank goodness none of you were around, as they would have seen you for sure," said Charlotte, looking pointedly at Fromage and remembering his reluctance to leave her by herself."

"They moved around like ghosts, hardly seeming to touch the ground. It was both thrilling and chilling watching them move about. I have to admit that I felt sick and afraid. They seemed so at ease, as if they were used to entering places in which they did not belong. Their movements seemed effortless."

Illustration 16: "A real Ninja Cat," according to Charlotte.

"They did not stay long where they were, as if they knew where they were going. They were sure footed and just slid into the banquet hall. There was no one in sight. I noticed that my paws were shaking and this made me angry at myself as I am normally not afraid."

"I slid out of my hiding place. The place was not well lit, and I shook off my anger due to feelings of nervousness. I followed them into the hall and hid behind a statue."

"The larger of the shadows pointed to a beam, and the Ninja Cat vaulted up there and released something which fell neatly into the hands of the human shadow below. The shadow swiftly placed the document behind an urn. Without hesitation or looking around they then disappeared into the night as if they were spirits."

"I had only enough energy to scuttle back under the carpet, with my heart thumping... I wouldn't want to meet those two on a lone night for sure," ended Charlotte.

We shook with excitement at the thought of meeting these shadowy figures. Fromage said, "I would have dealt with the Ninja Cat if I was to face-to-face with him, Charlotte."

Charlotte looked at him shaking her head. "No way, Fromage! I am glad you were not in the premises when they came in."

I suddenly came back to the present. We could deal with these mysterious shadowy creatures later on. We needed to see what was going on in the banquet hall. "Is there any way we can watch what is going on in the banquet hall?" I asked Charlotte.

"Yes, come on," she said. "I found a place on the first floor where we can see what is going on without being observed."

We quietly left our place under the stairs and raced after her. Fortunately, Missy and the servers were busy serving the guests in the hall and there was no one on the stairs. The party was still in full swing.

The most important part of what Charlotte had related was the fact that something was hidden behind an urn in the banquette hall. Surely, this couldn't be anything but the secret documents which had been placed for recovery by the Master Spy.

I said softly, "It appears that Charlotte witnessed something very important. The missing documents have been retrieved and placed in the hall for the Master Spy to collect at the party today."

There were urns placed all around the banquette hall. Charlotte shook her head in confusion. She looked at me apologetically. She just could not be sure which one of the urns the documents had been placed behind.

Seeing Charlotte's anxious face, I said, "Bravo Charlotte! You were brave to be left all alone and you have proved to be a very good spy. Let's see what goes on now."

We watched the proceedings quietly without moving. Missy and her team were smoothly weaving in out of the small clusters of guests offering them cheese and wine. Fromage observed with pride that the guests seemed to relish the delicious cheeses and the vintage wines that were being served.

My eyes were on Solo, as I wondered what he would do next. I ticked off in my head what I already knew from Terrance so far: Solo knew where the Master Spy was coming from. Did he suspect anyone in particular? Solo knew for sure that the documents would move out of the compound this evening, and I wondered what he would do to prevent it.

All the guests looked very distinguished, and Terrance had informed us that they were all important ambassadors with their spouses and other high level staff from various embassies.

It was strange! When Terrance first told us about spies, I had imagined a shadowy figure in a trench coat, his face hidden by a hat and dark glasses moving around as if in hiding. But everyone in the beautiful hall looked very polished. How would Solo accuse an ambassador or a high-level dignitary outright of stealing important documents? And which one of them was the Master Spy?

I don't know what the others were feeling. As for me, I could hardly breathe watching Solo move around the guests with ease, chatting first to one person and then to next. He finally stopped circulating and started speaking to a tall elegant gentleman.

The party was almost over, and the guests were starting to trickle out saying their thanks to the hostess, a petite French lady who was the French Ambassador, when Solo accidentally spilled his wine glass on the tall elegant gentleman.

I heard Monk's sharp intake of breath! He was mortified that Solo had made such a gaff. I whispered to him, "After all it was a simple accident."

Solo apologized profusely and mopped the gentleman's coat with a white handkerchief. Missy quietly came up to them with a large white serviette and dabbed the gentleman's jacket smoothly. The party went back to normal and everyone continued either talking among themselves or saying their goodbyes to each other and the French Ambassador.

Missy was back in a jiffy, the coat cleaned up. Cara added with pride, "Missy certainly knows her job to perfection."

The cocktail party soon ended and I wondered if Solo had seen the Master Spy. What about the strange figures Charlotte had seen last night? What were they up to in the French Embassy? Surely, they had to be linked to the case of the important documents, I thought.

It was too much of a coincidence that these shadowy frightening figures, as described by Charlotte, were in the compound for another matter the night before the cocktail party. What were they doing in the banquette hall? Obviously retrieving the document to place it at a more convenient place for recovery.

Brave Charlotte!

I shuddered to think how frightened she must have been observing these figures all by herself. I was glad she was coming home with us.

8 - Friend or Foe?

When the last guest left, we started on our way back home. Fromage excitedly informed Charlotte about meeting his twin brother, Camembert. He promised her that we would go to his place so he could introduce her to his brother.

I thought about what we had just witnessed. I wanted to find out what Solo knew so far and was impatient for Terrance to get whatever information he could by listening in on Solo's and Hobbs' conversation at work.

I felt strangely out of depth on this case. *Who were the strange figures that had entered the embassy, as observed by Charlotte?* My thoughts returned to this question again and again.

A sudden fear gripped me all at once, and I almost stopped jogging. This made Monk break quickly to avoid bumping in to me.

Could the Ninja Cat that Charlotte had observed be Camembert?

I dare not voice my thoughts! *Oh no!* I said to myself. Fromage would be very sad if his brother turned out to be part of a criminal gang. He was so proud of Camembert, talking non-stop about what an agile and elegant kitty he was. *What would his reaction be if Camembert turned out to be common crook, however sophisticated he was?*

I needed to get to the bottom of this pronto! I am very protective of my family and could not bear the thought of Fromage's dismay if his brother turned out to be disreputable.

I assured everyone loudly that we would visit Camembert tomorrow without fail to introduce him not only to Charlotte but also to Terrance and Polo.

Polo was eager to meet Camembert and ask him if he would be willing to give him a special performance. Polo felt really disappointed that he was the only doggy amongst his group who had not witnessed Camembert's acrobatic performance in the park.

We kitties hadn't either, and Fromage assured us with a wave of his hand: "Camembert will perform for you. I will ask him myself. I myself will show my own Ninja act to Camembert, perhaps he could learn a few moves from me."

We all looked at each other. There were shocked gasps from Cara and Charlotte and chuckles from the rest of us at this astounding smug statement! As I said before, Fromage has a very confident nature and he thinks the world of his own abilities.

He was oblivious to our shocked gasps and chuckles.

It was late when we got home and still later when Missy returned. I guessed that she had to be the last to leave. As the manager, she must ensure that the wine glasses and platters were cleared away and returned to our cheese restaurant. She was tired but happy!

The party had been an outstanding success and many others from the diplomatic circle had requested Missy's business card, asking her to visit them the following week to organize similar parties for them. With a contented sigh, pleased for Missy, we cuddled up in bed with her.

Everyone was quickly asleep after the day's activities. Only I had trouble sleeping, thinking of Camembert and wondering how Fromage would react if my suspicions proved to be true. I finally drifted off to sleep. But it was a restless slumber as I kept seeing the shadowy figures Charlotte had described.

***

Life looked better in the bright morning sunlight.

We had a leisurely breakfast and hung around with Missy as she was in no hurry to get to work. However, she had some bills to sort out and she left mid-morning on her rounds.

Monk and Polo had arrived by that time, and we set off to pay Camembert a visit. Monk whispered to me that Terrance had some news for us and he would meet us later this evening to let us know what he had found out. He could not join us to meet Camembert as he was at work with Solo.

Camembert seemed delighted to see us. Fromage took great pride in introducing his brother to Charlotte and Polo. On our previous visit, I had been too preoccupied to notice Camembert's surroundings. Now I could see the place was tastefully decorated, and there was nothing gaudy about it. The furniture was old but elegant.

Illustration 17: Fromage and Camembert! Can you tell them apart?

Camembert had without hesitation complied with Fromage's request to give us an acrobatic performance. The two brothers had one thing in common. They were both cocky and sure of themselves. I must admit that Camembert was a superb acrobat. He turned cartwheels and swung on and off high cupboards and doors like a graceful little monkey.

One major difference was that unlike his brother Fromage, he was not in the least bit clumsy. He steps were sure footed and graceful. He could pirouette like a ballerina.

Super-duper polished performance!

Fromage was declaring that he wanted to show Camembert his own skillful performance as Ninja Cat. To his surprise, he found that all his friends in unison said, "Later, Fromage, later. You don't want Camembert to have an inferior complex after watching you perform." That explanation convinced him and he settled down.

We were lying around Camembert's spacious kitchen after his fantastic performance, when a tall young lady entered the kitchen. She stopped when she saw her kitchen filled with fur balls. But she recovered from her surprise and said with a wide smile: "Good that you have made lots of friends, Camembert."

I could see that Camembert and his mistress had a very close relationship. They seemed to love each other very much and I was pleased for Fromage's brother. Both he and Fromage had found loving homes when they were separated from their parents.

I noticed how her long dark hair framed her high cheek bones. She was tall and lean and just like Camembert, extremely supple. Her face reminded me of a pretty fox, long, lean and smart with buttery large eyes.

Surely, I was wrong last night, suspecting them of being criminals. Felons invading homes to remove property not belonging to them. It couldn't be. Or stealing documents causing an international crisis.

In their sunlight filled kitchen, they looked like anything but crooks. They were warm and intelligent. The both of them. Camembert had an earnest and pleasant personality; he was less talkative than Fromage, but definitely charming and his companion seemed to be charming as well.

I could see that he was very happy to see Fromage again and he was very cordial towards Fromage's new family and friends.

We heard that Ivy, Camembert's friend and mistress was attached to the French Embassy as cultural officer. Together they had traveled the world promoting French culture in the different countries Ivy was posted by the Ministry of Foreign Affairs. Surely if Ivy was French and attached to the Embassy, she wouldn't cause any harm to it.

We invited Camembert to visit us soon and then took our leave.

9 - Family is Precious

Terrance met us in the garden and we scampered into the library, our usual meeting place. It had been an adventurous evening at the French Embassy, but I was anxious to hear from Terrance what Solo had to say.

Knowing our impatience, Terrance started immediately: "When Solo was hired, he had one major job to do. He would retrieve the stolen documents from the Master Spy before he left the premises and replace them with false documents."

"That was his assignment. He was not given any other details. All he knew was that the Master Spy should leave the premises with the false documents thinking that he had succeeded. He was provided with the name of the Master Spy."

"How on earth did he do that?" we all asked Terrance in unison.

"Terrance, we were watching every move he made," I added.

Terrance gave a wide grin. "Solo has his methods," he responded.

Light bulbs suddenly flashed. Eureka! I realized how he did it! I remember Solo spilling wine on the elegant gentleman. I had thought he had done so by accident. But it was on purpose. I explained to Monk and the others what I believed had happened.

"Solo created a deviation! That's how he did it. While wiping the wine off, his nimble fingers took the documents off his jacket."

"You are a smart kitty! Inca," said Terrance. "But yesterday, he had a little help from a friend," continued Terrance with a twinkle in his eyes.

I thought back to what had happened at the party. I saw in my mind's eye Solo spilling the wine, apologizing and wiping the wine with his handkerchief. Then I saw Missy approaching him immediately, a large white serviette in her hand, helping the elegant gentleman out of his jacket and coming back a little later with it cleaned up.

I grinned with delight and said "Our Missy helped him, didn't she? It was she who quickly switched the envelopes, wasn't it?"

"Yes, indeed," replied Terrance.

We were wild with delight! The members of my family broke in to a wild jig, dancing with glee at the thought of our very own Missy helping Solo avoid an international crisis. Missy had detective blood in her genes too! She hadn't mentioned a word to any of us, and I saw Cara starting to pout when she realized this.

"Come on, Cara; let's just be proud of Missy's actions. She was in no danger after all; we were all there to protect her," I said. This made Cara timidly smile at me and nod in agreement.

I didn't add that I never told Missy half the things we were up to, so *why should she tell us everything?* But this piece I kept to myself as Cara was already appeased. But we still hadn't solved all the mystery. *Who were the shadowy figures that Charlotte had followed in to the banquette hall? What was their role in this saga?*

I made Charlotte relate the story of her vigil in the deserted embassy the night we left her there to spy.

Charlotte—in the security of the library in the midst of all her friends—related the story as she had told us. This time with no fear in her voice as she felt safe among friends.

After she had finished, we sat thinking, deep in thought, when she squeaked in a small voice, "Fromage, please don't be upset with me. But something has been worrying me since we visited Camembert."

I knew my suspicions had proved to be correct but how would Fromage react? Charlotte was Fromage's dearest friend, but would even such a bond be able to cope with what she had to say?

I remained silent and looked at Fromage, who responded, "Charlotte, I trust you. Please say what is on your mind."

Charlotte said: "When I met Ivy, I could not help but recognize the soft smell of lavender floating in the air. I have been struggling to recall where I had smelt this fragrance. Was it my memory of our last trip to Provence? I kept asking myself."

Of course, Provence is famous for its fields of lavender resembling a plush purple carpet from a distance. We had been in Provence a few months ago solving another mystery. I could well understand Charlotte's confusion.

She continued: "But then I realized this was the scent I smelt from the great shadow when she entered the French Embassy. The human shadow that slid into the Embassy with the Ninja Cat after you left me.... I am sorry Fromage, but I am certain it was Ivy and Camembert who were the shadows, resembling the ghosts of Cat Woman and Ninja Cat."

There was a stunned silence in the library. Charlotte is a perspective little hamster. I knew she wouldn't get this wrong. She doesn't speak lightly. We all trusted her judgment. No one said a word, waiting for Fromage's reaction.

For once in his young life, Fromage didn't seem to know what to say. The usually garrulous Fromage was struck dumb, and out of habit, he crept up to me and put his head on my shoulder. I knew he believed Charlotte. I guess he too had been suspecting what I had but didn't dare put it in words.

I was his big sister, and since the day I met him, had made him feel better whenever he had any problems, be it his loneliness at parting from his family or when Missy first decided to cross over from Paris to London and he wanted to find a solution to not leaving Charlotte behind.

The silence continued and everyone was sad watching Fromage in my arms.

Cara came quickly and hugged the both of us and Charlotte had tears silently dripping down her little face. She crept in to his scarf and nuzzled his neck comfortingly.

Terrance and Monk were not used to emotional outbreaks, having a typical tough British exterior, and they believed in keeping a stiff upper lip. But I could see that they were dismayed also.

Polo broke the silence with an excitable yap.

"Inca, you have to talk to Camembert." If he really is a villain, he has to change his ways. Even bad kitties can be converted to good kitties, can't they?"

Illustration 18: Terrance and Monk trying to hide their dismay!

"Out of the mouths of babes, so says the famous saying," meowed Monk comparing Polo to a babe.

Of course, Polo was right. Why hadn't I thought of it myself? I should have done so as soon as my suspicions were aroused. I would go immediately to see Camembert and speak to him. There was no other way out.

"Cara, please take Fromage and Charlotte home," I said. "I will be back soon!"

Without another word, I raced from the library and started pounding the streets lightly, practically flying in my haste to get to Camembert's home. After a few minutes, I realized that I was not alone. Monk and Terrance had asked the others to go home. They had decided not to let me go alone and were following close at my heels. Loyal friends to the end!

The house was in darkness when we arrived. It looked as if everyone was fast asleep. But that did not change my mind. I was determined to corner Camembert and get him to spill the beans. I needed to know what was going on, and pronto!

I went to the back window and started scratching at it with my paws. Monk jumped up beside me and added his rat-tat to mine. We were making enough noise to wake the dead. So, it was no surprise that a light switched on upstairs and I heard Ivy's voice say, "What on earth is going on?"

We heard her voice and saw Camembert peeping out the window. He was out of the house through Ivy's upstairs window in a jiffy. He swung through the window as easily as he would walk down a staircase and landed besides Terrance.

We saw Ivy's head peer out, and noticing that it was only us, Camembert's friends, she waved to us and put off the lights.

"Hi, what's up?" Camembert asked.

"Coming to attack my gourmet croquettes again," he said with a cheeky grin, which petered out when he saw our serious faces. "Has anything happened to Fromage?" he asked, his face growing long again.

"Let's have a talk, Camembert," I responded.

I asked Monk and Terrance to give us some space. Then I took Camembert to a corner and sat him down. He did so without a word. It was as if he had accepted me as his big sister, same as Fromage. I calmly related what was our concern and how upset

Fromage was and then sat waiting for an explanation.

Camembert had gone silent. We sat for a long moment looking at each other. My eyes boring into his in accusation, and his looking at me pleading.

At last he stuttered, "It's not as you imagine it, Inca." I can explain, but trust me "It's not as you think it is."

He looked so genuine that I paused to think. I reminded myself that I was a real detective now. I had been involved in several cases.

What would Solo have done in these circumstances?

"Don't jump to conclusions, think the case through," I said to myself. That's what Solo would have done. Thoughtfully stroking my beautiful whiskers, I reflected on the case. Those who recruited Solo already knew that the documents would be picked up by the Master Spy at the party. That was a fact!

How did they know that? Obviously because they had it put there themselves.

Then why did they ask Solo to switch the documents?

Slowly I had a feeling I was getting to the bottom of it. I looked at Camembert once again.

Why was he unable to talk and explain himself?

Because he and Ivy were good spies. On the same side as Solo. They were double agents pretending to help the other side.

"Camembert, we are family now. You can trust me. Tell me the truth please."

Camembert, decided to come clean and the whole story poured out. Ivy had been tasked to promise the Master Spy the documents. She had deliberately stolen the documents and hidden them where it could be collected by the Master Spy when he attended the reception. She did this with the help of Camembert.

The Master Spy then took the documents and it was up to Solo to ensure that he replaced the documents with false documents before he left the party, taking the suspicion off Ivy.

Spies and counter spies galore, this spy business was complicated. I was glad it was over and Camembert and Ivy were not thieves.

Returning home with Monk and Terrance, I told them what I had learned. This is good news for Fromage said Monk while Terrance nodded his large head in agreement.

The group was anxiously waiting for our return. Polo had not returned home either. When I told them the truth, there was a huge sigh of relief. I looked at Fromage in silence.

"Thank you, Inca," he said.

It had been a great shock for him, but everything was back to normal. His little world was complete. He could count on his family and his friends. He had found his brother again. A brother he could be proud of, a brother who was an international spy and a true Ninja cat!

We had all learned a lesson: Family is precious!

That night we were invited to Camembert's place to spend the evening. We gathered together at his residence and found to our delight that Ivy had laid out Ninja costumes for every one of us, starting with the smallest, Charlotte, to the largest, Terrance.

We donned our attire with pride and made make believe that we were all real Ninjas!

Hee Yaah!

Illustration 19: We are all Ninja Spy Cats!

The End

Illustrations

Made in the USA
Middletown, DE
11 February 2020